Elephant Rides Again

First published 2005
Evans Brothers Limited
2A Portman Mansions
Chiltern Street
London W1U 6NR

British Library Cataloguing in Publication Data
Harrison, Paul, 1969-
        Elephant rides again. - (Twisters)
        1. Children's stories - Pictorial works
        I. Title
        823.9'2 [J]

ISBN-10: 0237530740
13-digit ISBN (from 1 January 2007) 9780237530747

Printed in China by WKT Company Limited

Series Editor: Nick Turpin
Design: Robert Walster
Production: Jenny Mulvanny
Series Consultant: Gill Matthews

Elephant Rides Again

Paul Harrison
and Liz Million

Evans

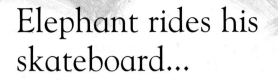

Elephant rides his
skateboard...

...along the street...

6

...to the path...

...and down the hill.

The skateboard went faster
and faster and faster.

"Look out!"

BANG!

16

17

Up, up, up...

...down,
down,
  down.

CRASH!

"Owww, my head."

"I'm never going
skateboarding again."

"Hold on.
What's over there?"

"Roller skates!"

Why not try reading another Twisters book?